A NOTE TO PARENTS

Reading Aloud with Your Child

Research shows that reading books aloud is the single most valuable support parents can provide in helping children learn to read.

- Be a ham! The more enthusiasm you display, the more your child will enjoy the book.
- Run your finger underneath the words as you read to signal that the print carries the story.
- Leave time for examining the illustrations more closely; encourage your child to find things in the pictures.
- Invite your youngster to join in whenever there's a repeated phrase in the text.
- Link up events in the book with similar events in your child's life.
- If your child asks a question, stop and answer it. The book can be a means to learning more about your child's thoughts.

Listening to Your Child Read Aloud

The support of your attention and praise is absolutely crucial to your child's continuing efforts to learn to read.

- If your child is learning to read and asks for a word, give it immediately so that the meaning of the story is not interrupted. DO NOT ask your child to sound out the word.
- On the other hand, if your child initiates the act of sounding out, don't intervene.
- If your child is reading along and makes what is called a miscue, listen for the sense of the miscue. If the word "road" is substituted for the word "street," for instance, no meaning is lost. Don't stop the reading for a correction.
- If the miscue makes no sense (for example, "horse" for "house"), ask your child to reread the sentence because you're not sure you understand what's just been read.
- Above all else, enjoy your child's growing command of print and make sure you give lots of praise. *You are your child's first teacher—and the most important one. Praise from you is critical for further risk-taking and learning.*

—Priscilla Lynch
Ph.D. New York University
Educational Consultant

To Elana Saxe
—S.C.

To Bob and Maggi,
who held onto their sense of humor
in spite of everything
—M.D.R.

Library of Congress Cataloging-in-Publication Data

Calmenson, Stephanie.
My dog's the best / by Stephanie Calmenson ; illustrated by Marcy Dunn Ramsey.
p. cm.—(Hello reader! Level 1)
"Cartwheel Books."
Summary: Their owners describe a variety of dogs, smooth, shaggy, friendly, and fast.
ISBN 0-590-33072-1
[1. Dogs—Fiction. 2. Pets—Fiction.] I. Ramsey, Marcy Dunn, ill.
II. Title. III. Series.
PZ7.C136Mye 1997
[E]—DC21 97-9726
CIP
AC

10 9 8 7

Printed in the U.S.A. 24

First printing, September 1997

My Dog's the Best!

by Stephanie Calmenson
Illustrated by Marcy Dunn Ramsey

Hello Reader!—Level 1

Cartwheel BOOKS®
SCHOLASTIC INC.
New York Toronto London Auckland Sydney

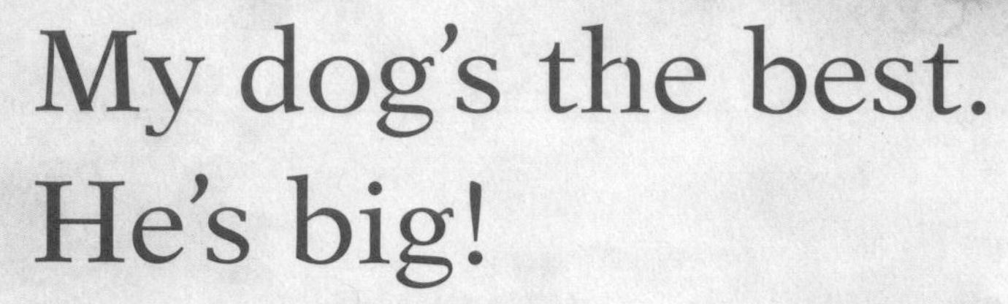

My dog's the best.
He's big!

My dog's the best.
She's small.

My dog's the best.
She's short.

My dog's the best.
He's tall.

My dog's the best.
No, *my* dog's the best.

No, ***my*** dog's better than yours!

My dog's the best.
She's smooth.

My dog's the best.
He's shaggy.

My dog's the best.
She's got a pompon
on her tail.

My dog's the best.
Her tail is waggy.

My dog's the best.
She hugs me.

My dog's the best.
He licks.

My dog's the best.
He protects me.

My dog's the best.
She does tricks.

My dog's the best.
No, *my* dog's the best.

No, ***my*** dog's better than yours!

My dog's the best.
He's fast!

My dog's the best.
She's slow.

My dog's the best.
He's silly!

My dog's the best.
She's for show.

My dog's the best.
Hear her bark!

My dog's the best.
Hear him whine.

My dog's the best.

No, *my* dog's the best!

No, ***my*** dog's the best!

My dog's the best because he's *mine!*

I'm
the best!